Maudlin Memories

with BonnieAnn

ISBN:978-1-927914-54-0

Photo by Matt Mattera

Graphic Design by Jared Strouse

This book is a work of fiction. Names, characters, places and incidents either are products of the author's imagination or are used fictitiously. Any resemblance to actual events or locales or persons is intended for fictional purposes.

Published by Flower Publishing
Montreal, Canada

In memory of my blessed mother, Miriam and my father, John, who taught me to appreciate all art forms and to constantly explore my inner creative nature; who insisted on perfect elocution, articulation, and spelling; who taught me to love, share, believe in myself, and to never settle for unfulfilled goals or dreams. To my son, David, who believes in me and supports all of my endeavors and to his wife Colleen for her sensitivity and enthusiasm. To my mother's namesake, my daughter, Miriam who has worked tirelessly to bring my dream to fruition and to her husband Gino who has become like another son to me. To my sister, Joyce and my brother, Roland who have guided my life like a second set of parents. And finally to my first husband and my current husband who have accepted my faults and weaknesses throughout fifty years of emotional peaks and valleys. To all of you: "Thank you for the memories."

Introduction

BRAIN: briefly defined by Webster's Dictionary as a noun: "nerve tissue enclosed in the cranium."

MEMORY; Roget's Thesaurus (or as a student once asked me, "do you have one of those Roger they saw us books?"): remembrance, retention, tenacity, readiness, reminiscence, recognition, recurrence, recollection, reminder, memento, souvenir, keepsake, relic, memorandum, memorabilia, tenacious."

MAUDLIN: Webster's Dictionary: an adjective; sentimental.

SENTIMENTAL: Webster's Dictionary: adjective: very special, emotional

In researching the importance of memory for the purpose of giving some credibility to my book, beyond the obvious: a happy, easy, quick read; I became compelled to understand what part of the brain is devoted to memories and how important memories are to us from birth to death. I am a layperson with no medical training in neurology. Like most of us, I have experienced looking at pictures of the brain in school health textbooks, posters on a doctor's wall, even colorful graphics presented in an instructional infomercial promoting relief of pain, sleeplessness, and memory loss.

While experiencing an "episode" related to one of my many unknown health conditions, I had the excitement of viewing my own MRI during which time my neurologist explained, in layman's language, the myriad of complexities of my brain. Yes there was the proverbial "gray matter," "white matter," and several terms that did not matter to me at the time. The important information that stayed in my memory was: everything looked normal! I did not have cancer, I had not had a stroke, and I had no other deformity in my brain which would cut my life short, or perhaps lead to early dementia. So one would think, being as normal as my tests showed, I would leave the MRI experience far behind to move on to my "happy" place. Indeed I did. However, my lifelong devotion to memories started to take a demanding place in my daily life.

Once given the privilege of seeing inside my own cranium, I was driven to explore memory functions and to discover why my unique memories have served me as a respite from all negative experiences in my life. I wanted to discover how they enabled me to escape from moments of sadness, fear, and low self esteem to a spa-like place of peace and healing. I needed to understand the power of memories and their ability to give me the strength I often needed to move past the momentary problems in my life.

For me, memories are euphoric, transcending and spiritual. I must now share with you how I got to this place. My family had a city home and a country cottage. My mother was pregnant with me when our country home, "Singing Hills" was purchased. My nineteen year old brother was entering WWII; my sister was 16 and preparing for graduation from high school. I was a "change of life baby." In spite of the age of my parents and the large difference in age between me and my siblings, we were a devoted, happy family. My arrival brought joy to my mother and father and love and fascination from my brother and sister. As we endured air raids and blackouts, lack of fuel and provisions during the progression of WWII, my mother rocked me by the fireplace in our city home and her tears for my brother's safety fell warm upon my baby cheeks. That may be my first memory; followed by my sister playing the piano and daddy playing the saxophone. It seems that even way back then, I felt the sadness of the times but somehow my memories are of the joy of my family loving me so much, the warmth of the fire, the comfort of music, and the ethereal promise of the final reward for life's labors.

Picture this: a country cottage, with no electricity. An outhouse decorated with curtains, fresh flowers, books and magazines for quiet learning and reflection. Lanterns shiny and full of fuel ready to light when an after dinner, after dark, visit was necessary for the relief of bodily functions. Whip-poor-wills, calling in the distance, deer making twilight visit to the apple trees in the meadow. The old hand pump cranking in the kitchen sink as Mother pumped up another pot of well water. It had to be heated on the old black wood/kerosene stove to boil water for dish washing. Meanwhile one of the men slipped off to the cellar to raid the wooden ice chest and retrieve a few cold brews for the after dinner card game. I can hear Mother calling out, "don't forget to chop some ice for lemonade!"

There were chores to be done because even then, Memorial Day was recognized as the unofficial beginning of summer, and crops had to be tended which meant these farm children could not dilly-dally too long enjoying recreation.

As a teenage boy, dad joined the Navy during WWI. His view of the world was expanded far beyond his humble beginnings in Russellville. After seven Voyages to France on the Matsonia he returned home an honored Veteran. During his adult life he marched into many cemeteries as a man, stepping proudly beside VFW comrades every Memorial Day, yes even with Drum and Bugle corps, and yes he was the "drummer man" when needed, but basically dad was a fiddle/saxophone man.

Over the years, our family celebrated by planting crops, walking to the local cemetery to watch dad in the parade, decorating the graves of loved ones, returning home for a feast of the usual, hamburgers, hot dogs, watermelon, iced tea, lemonade, cookies, cake; and as age allowed, the spirit of our choice. So many things have changed during the past one hundred years. As I watch television news reports, read events in the newspaper, and listen to friends and neighbors discuss their plans for Memorial Day, some traditions never change. As the saying goes, "if it isn't broken, don't fix it!"   However, I have no lilac blossoms. They bloomed a month ago. Guess our climate has changed!

Preface

Welcome to Maudlin Memories. Think of it like sharing your favorite recipe with no cooking or trips to the grocery store for supplies and never any failures. Each reflection suggests a "memory" for discussion amongst the generations of your family.

My son feels the word "maudlin" suggests sadness. Webster describes the word as meaning "sentimental." We all have happy and sad memories. My dedication to this section is "let's take a sentimental journey". Let us keep it "soft and fluffy". Wherever our journey takes us may we feel joyful that we still have memories at our journey's end.

In this electronic age, how peaceful not to worry :*did we plug in our chargers* to communicate? but only to pull out an old photograph, close our eyes and remember, the way we were. Our memory banks will charge on their own. If you cannot afford a relaxing manicure, pedicure, rely on your mental "spa". Close your eyes, breathe deeply, and enjoy the soothing therapy of your memories. Allow the soft, warm bubbles of the hot tub in your thoughts to cleanse and refresh you.

For those of you who can enjoy something"sappy" only when it is maple syrup on a pile of hot pancakes served at your local sugar house in the spring- or one of Denny's monthly specials -this column may not be for you.

For those who enjoy the black and white version of Casablanca, looking through the scrapbook or photo album, reminiscing about your child's first birthday, your mom and dad's 50th anniversary. Being "mother of the bride, or the groom". Remembering the first time you saw the ocean. Still admiring a stone you collected on a hiking trip or the pieces of sea glass you found at the beach. Your wedding album, Your first camping trip when it rained so hard, the tent collapsed. The raccoons ran off with the hot dogs and the skunk marked his territory. The sleeping bags displayed a growth of mold. But you laughed anyway, and thought maybe camping is not for me. The first comic book you remember. The original colors in a box of Crayola crayons. Your first wagon, bicycle or other means of independent transportation. Your first kiss. The first dollar you earned. The first person to say "I love you".

If any of the above tapped your memory banks. And gave you that "feel good" moment, this column may be for you. We might as well start at the beginning and take a journey together to the enchanting land of memories.

My first memory of "independent transportation" was my little red wagon. It was shiny and wonderful, but, someone had to pull me or I had to straddle and use my feet. Steering was a problem, plus no brakes and worn out shoe soles. Next came my tricycle. Wow, what a feeling of freedom as I rode along the sidewalks in my neighborhood in Springfield. Wind in my face, braids flying behind.. but I was outgrowing my transportation. Next came my Columbia balloon tire, with training wheels, bicycle. Now I could leave my street and ride to the park. Oh, the freedom once again. I never did outgrow the training wheels. I am off balance.

Now at 69, I have been gifted with an adult tricycle. Oh the fears of hand brakes, will I tip over? can I peddle uphill with no gears Guess what?, day by day I am learning once again and with each ride on my adult Trike, the old memories of my little red wagon surround me. Now new memories are developing.

Part One

Eclectic Electric

Pressure Cooker

Do You Feel Lucky?

Eclectic Electric

Newspapers

Brilliant Scholars

Part Two

To Every Thing There is a Season

Sugar Plums

Wait for it

Winter in New England

Hearts and Flowers

Memorial Day

Mother's Day

Think Plastic

Fireworks

Summer in New England

Part Three

Memory Soil

Long Island Boys

BFFs

Road Rage

Laugh Lines- with Guest Writer Miriam Proctor Tedesco

Making it to the Olympics

Part Four

A Bit of Whimsy

Theatre

Content

Year of the Zombie

Disclaimers

Part Five

Red Sandals

Part Six

The Afterglow

Part One

Eclectic Electric

Eclectic Electric

Like the decorating of my home, reader's choice is always eclectic! I find that ELECTRIC! My dad, an electrician frequently used the old fashioned and NOT recommended test for power by touching an outlet with his finger. Wow! Dad loved the "spark" and found it exhilarating. So dear readers, your eclectic memories light up my life! Let's plug in!

Marcia from Hampshire County turned my lights on with her luminous memory. A different kind of a "trip". In childhood she loved dancing. She so wanted to become a ballerina. Her physical presentation did not lend itself to that dance. She then tried tap dancing. She will never forget her first pair of shiny tap shoes. She was so excited until the metal taps slipped instead of clicked across a hardwood floor. Down she went. Up she came with a sprained ankle. Not giving up, Marcia was satisfied with square dancing. She remembers those golden nights in hill town halls when the floor vibrated beneath your feet as the fiddle, piano and drums pounded out the rhythm and the prompter called out "circle eight hands around. Honor your corner lady, honor your partners all, swing that corner lady and promenade the hall" Dive for the oyster, dive for the clam, dive for your home in the happy land." Bright colored cotton skirts swinging to every beat. Ballerina flats ready to hold the floor through the wildest swing any young man could bring on. And some of those boys were so strong you would think they were roping a bull! Long hair flying, cheeks flushing as the perspiration reached levels beyond the control of "secret;" all day preparing for the Saturday night dance. Who would take her to the dance? Who would ask her for a dance? And after all the fast footwork, who would ask her for a waltz? Close, cozy, gentle and pure.

And so it was that on a winter night in a town hall in the New England hills, after a game and maple sugar on snow supper, Marcia waltzed her night away and soon, she married her true love. As years passed, family grown, grandchildren filling her life, Marcia needed to dance again. She surprised her husband with lessons at Arthur Murray studios at the X in Springfield. It was a long trip once a week but they were both committed to sharing the joy of "the dance" once again. They mastered the ballroom dances. Took a cruise and won first prize for their dance expertise.

Pressure Cooker

Contributors express to me that remembering something that once was part of everyday life, mostly harmless, and brought great joy, gives them peace and helps them deal with the unanswered questions of our current world. Contributors asked to remain anonymous because the subject matter is fragile in the aftermath of current events. I will simply refer to Mem1, etc. Our world has frequently been described as a pressure cooker.

Mem 1: "Mother, {a 14 year old asking} what is a pressure cooker?" Is it for food? Oh yes, my mother, your grandmother, made chicken and dumplings for our family every Sunday night when I was growing up." It was so tasty and made us feel loved and comfortable!" Do we own one? No. Why, I use a crock pot and I never make chicken and dumplings." Why? I never asked Grandma for her recipe." Mem 2: When I was a girl my mother made pot roast in a pressure cooker. The tender meat and the sumptuous gravy!" I asked, Do you own one now? No, I don't make pot roast, too much red meat!" Mem 3: "Dad why do people carry those pressure things in a backpack if they are used for cooking?" Response: "Son, we need to talk. Every backpack is not carrying a pressure cooker; I need to know your concerns about the backpack and the pressure cooker". A lengthy discussion ensued. Mem4: Grandson: "Gramps,:

When kids come to school with a backpack and they act funny, what should I do? " Response:" "in my day we only carried a lunch bag and a book strap". "School kids today use back packs because they have so many books to carry for homework and other assignments. "If you feel uncomfortable about something, talk to your teacher and your parents." Grandson: "Gramps:" what would you do if you saw a backpack that looked big? Response:"I told you no one had a backpack in my day. What we brought to school was as I said. I am certain no one had a pressure cooker in their lunch sack!" Aileen shared that in Nova Scotia over sixty years ago some folks made alcoholic beverages in a pressure cooker. If someone lost track of time and temperature, *bing, bang*, yes an explosion erupted! No one hurt, just the loss of alcohol spilled on the ceiling and the floor. Mel following in her grandmother's and mother's footsteps, still makes the famous family baked beans, for her church, in a modern pressure cooker.

Memory 5: My brother presented my mother with a pig's head to make head cheese. She had a deep well pressure cooker in her old I940"s gas stove. The temperature was too high, she was doing laundry; *bing, bang* the lid blew off and pig parts attached to the floor and ceiling. Mother had a terrible clean up and daddy and brother worried about what had been wasted. Fertilizer another disaster in the past week, with many injuries and chaos. Mem 5: Like clockwork, every spring, a lady from Russell called the local State Senator; her complaint was her neighbor spreading fertilizer on his field abutting her home. She said the odor was so dreadful it would surely kill her.

In those days there were no laws to prohibit the spreading of fertilizer in her particular zoning area. She was angry and felt abused by society and the system. The gentle farmer was only trying to produce crops for sustenance. The Senator always found a compromise between the lady's anger and the farmer's right to survive. Boston born Will Durant was quoted as saying, "Civilization begins with order, grows with liberty, and dies with chaos" Hopefully our memories will help us keep order, our inherent knowledge will continue to guide us to liberty, and all of the above will keep us from chaos. Fear Not! We are a Nation Undivided!

Do You Feel Lucky?

Was it Clint Eastwood in "Dirty Harry" who asked that famous question, "Do you feel lucky?" {My personal choice of subject matter for this column} At a convenience store a few days after the beginning of 2012, I met a chap I have known for years but have not seen recently. After exchanging greetings, he expressed that he was waiting to check his lottery numbers. Because I continue to be annoyingly curious about humanity, I seized the moment and began drilling the poor chap with questions about the lottery and" luck". He does believe in luck, both good and bad. Throughout his lifetime he has experienced both. The Lottery? yes he has had his share of small luck. He believes in the "luck of the draw". He will continue to "play the game of chance". I then wound backwards in my memory banks to my first knowledge of good luck. Four leaf clovers! I found the first of hundreds, during my lifetime, at about age 6, outside our porch at our summer home "Singing Hills". I ran to my mother with great excitement to show her this amazing discovery! She said it was "good luck". I saw this like a family of four, but we were five. In a few days I found a five leaf clover. Now it all made sense, I would have all the luck I would ever need in a loving family. My mother "pressed" my clovers between the pages of one of my favorite bedtime books, "Poems for the Children's Hour". Those who have known me for years have patiently endured my search for four leaf clovers. I sense one is near and "pluck" it, to the amazement of those around me. Am I lucky?, not so much. I, like many other folks, do not believe in a "random act of luck". Do I love four leaf clovers? only for their beauty!

Dave from Huntington strongly feels that all good fortune is about blessings. When I asked him if he believed luck was about working, ethics, fate, determination, he simply said "it is all about blessings!"

John B. from Chester intrigued me with the sincerity in his voice and direct eye contact with me, when I asked him about luck. His response: "There is no such thing as luck or chance. You must do stuff to make things change."

A special lady from the South, recalled a memory of "good luck". She was a college student, working as an intern in a dental office, making $1.50 an hour. Her 1960 Chevy Malibu had threadbare tires and she needed safe transportation to college and work. On a rare day with a few hours off from school and work, her dad took her to the local racetrack. She had but $2.00 to place a bet. She bet on a horse with a name that enticed her. Before her race was over she had to leave the track to attend an evening class, not knowing if she was a winner or a loser. The next day her dad arrived at her workplace, smiling from ear to ear. He handed her sixty dollars, just the right amount to replace her tires. She was a winner, she says it was luck!

My husband was checking out at the store. The register total appeared and he was $5.00 short. The kind register clerk politely asked if he wished to return some items. Before he could answer a gentle stranger next in line, said" no he doesn't need to return anything, please sir accept my $5.00. " When my husband offered to take her name and address and return the money, she said, "please just do the same for someone else when you can." Luck or Blessing? I believe in blessings.

Newspapers

How Deeeee! It is good to be back in print. Thank you for your calls, cards and letters. Yes, I am still old and upright. You know the drill, when there is space Maudlin Memories will have a place. The only trouble with a three week hiatus at my age is I may have "forgotten" where I left off with my readers. I am on it, wait for it: Memories of newspapers.

LR from Chester shared his memory of interaction with newspapers by sharing the story of being a boy scout. In his small town scouts went door to door in wind , rain or snow, collecting discarded newspapers, filling their bike baskets, wagons, duffle bags, trash bags, with as many old newspapers as possible. Once the collection was complete, an adult had to transport the papers to a recycling destination and collect cash to be returned to the local Boy Scout Troop in an effort to keep this troop safe from financial extinction for a short period of time.

Sophie from Berkshire County wrote, "I could not imagine running my on line business without having old newspaper in which to safely wrap my products for mailing." Brenda says she cannot conduct a tag sale without piles of newspaper to wrap and protect the items she sells. Margaret tells of using newspaper to line old windows to shelter from winter winds when she was a child, and also piled on her rope bed as a mattress. I am amazed! I had no idea where this memory of newspapers would take us!

As promised, I dedicate this column to a man known as Wad. Fourteen years with the Spfld. Union, covering the night shift police beat from 8PM to 4AM. Mob hits, murders, a tough city in the 1950's. In 1961 "Wad" escaped the city and founded the Dalton-Hinsdale News. It was a weekly, conventional printing for a couple of years and then it was the first newspaper in the country to switch to offset printing. Using Crane's Distaff Linen for paper. I t was a stiff, super white paper. Photos came out clear as a bell. Yes, Crane's in Dalton, the firm that makes paper for currency for US, Canada, Mexico, Taiwan, and Brazil. Also banknote paper and all the stationery for Congress and the White House. The Dalton-Hinsdale News was mostly a family style paper, birthdays, the good news of the town. High school sports. Very little of the type of news he covered in Springfield. The record for the size of the paper was 48 pages. The one time he touched on national news was the Kennedy assassination and that was "front page." Three times a week a long drive was required to Canaan, Ct. Monday to the printer, Tuesday for the front page, allowing an opportunity for any last minute changes. Wednesday to pick the papers up to be delivered to the various vendors. One of those vendors was the Middlefield General Store, "Oldes General Store" in those days. In a vintage 50's vehicle it was often a treacherous journey through some raging blizzards in winter, seasonal flooded roads, dirt roads, wash outs, high winds, ice, sleet. In the hill towns in those days roadways were unpredictable and cars were not made as they are in 2012. But somehow the man known as "Wad" delivered the news each week. After his many years as a police beat reporter, he fulfilled his dream and published a paper quite free of crime and dedicated to hill town families. My deepest thanks to David Pierce for taking the time to share this special memory of Wadsworth Pierce.

Brilliant Scholars

Throughout time it has been said that we control our own destiny. Brilliant scholars, therapists, clergy, and even our own parents may have planted this thought within us. Do we truly believe this? Is it easier to think that our lives are driven by fate alone? That perhaps we are somehow rendered helpless to control the daily trials and tribulations of our lives because what will be, will be? Also, how much of what we see, read, or hear affects our daily decisions about our personal destiny? We all know the old saying, "jack of all trades, and master of none". In a New Year's Eve ball drop, that sums up BonnieAnn! I have been told that I am cognizant in a variety of areas. I have still not "mastered" the art of life! Each year as the clock strikes twelve on New Year's Eve, we all decide to change our destiny for the new year.

Resolutions often include better health habits, weight loss, more time being involved philanthropically within our communities, more quality time with our families, a new budget, a long overdue household repair, or perhaps just the ability to tidy up our space and stop the clutter. Perhaps take dancing lessons with our mate, or maybe learn to crochet or knit, or learn to play an instrument. Oh yes, I can talk the talk, but I cannot walk the walk. I gave up on New Year's resolutions years ago. Why? If you were paying attention you got the point I am not the master of anything. Frankly it is exhausting trying to keep all of these promises to myself. Do I think I have a "free pass" to destiny or fate? No!, I can only say, as I said about my Christmas cards, I will try to do better in 2013.

Reader Agnes shared her memory of a resolution as follows: "I wanted to de-clutter my house, but I also needed to lose weight and shape up before I had the ability to de-clutter." I ordered a blow-up type device, complete with an instructional CD. "I was so excited watching for the UPS truck to arrive in my driveway in five to ten business days." I just knew this was a good resolution and by spring I would be a shapely, healthy woman with a very neat home" Finally the device arrived {in fourteen days.} It had a foot pump included to inflate the apparatus. I think I lost five pounds just trying to pump it up. Then came the problem of sharing the family room television with my husband so I could watch the CD and perform my exercise routines professionally. After reading all of the written instructions, getting the stupid thing blown up, installing the CD in the television, I jumped on! The thing deflated I fell over and sprained my wrist". Needless to say after Agnes made a trip to the emergency room, waited for over an hour and returned home with another "apparatus" on her wrist, she lost interest in her resolutions. The exercise blow up is now another piece of clutter.

A channel from the UK started broadcasting in the United States in July. It is a down sliding auction dealing with genuine gemstones. It is addictive because it is also instructional. The point here is for

New Year's Eve they are promoting genuine gemstone butterflies. The premise is the metamorphosis of the butterfly from chrysalis to moth to a beautiful creature. The English people believe we should evolve each New Year as does the butterfly. When I get my wings, I will let you know.

Part Two

To Every Thing There is a Season

Sugar Plums

With the joy of the holiday season well underway, it is not surprising that "Reader's Choice" submissions this week are sparkling, glittering and twinkling with celebratory memories. Soon it will be "The Night Before Christmas." After weeks of exhausting preparation, the culmination of another year of hopes, dreams and visions of sugar plums dancing in our heads, and don't forget the prancing and pawing of each little hoof. As a child I was enthralled with that famous Christmas story. Each year on Christmas Eve, before "I lay me down to sleep," a designated family member had to read the wondrous tale. After I went to bed the "adults" had another version, not acceptable for young ears. The laughter and cacophony accompanying that version echoed up the stairs to my bedroom, and being a very nosey child, I was more consumed with what I was missing than with my simple "task" of going to sleep and waiting for Santa. For me the night before Christmas has always been drifting off to sleep with the sounds of family, friends, love, laughter and music. Church midnight services became part of my older years. Gifts on Christmas morning are indeed special, but if there are none, the joy of the "night before" will forever be my perfect present.

Carl's Christmas Eve memories are about a rural area where he grew up, with only a dirt road leading from his home to a small town and the church. The Christmas Eve church pageant was the highlight of the year. The presentation was complete with beautiful wide-eyed children, trying to remember their lines, their entrances and places, live animals, music, simple staging, costumes and decorations handcrafted by the local farm families. Carl played a variety of parts during his young years, including playing the part of one of the Three Wise Men. After the pageant the family returned to home. Sometimes Santa had already stopped by, other times he did not come until Christmas morning. A large box was always wrapped and ready for Carl. Each year a dear neighbor ripped up multiple pieces of newspaper, wadded them up and put them in the box. In one paper wad was a shiny silver dollar. Carl remembers his Christmas Eve as a child, not about gifts, rather the joy of the night, and that shiny silver dollar, to be searched for!

Speaking of the Wise Men, a wonderful lady shared a story. What if the Three Wise Men had been women? First they would have arrived on time because they would have asked for directions. Second, they would have thoroughly cleaned the manger before the blessed birth. Third, they would have brought practical gifts. You go girls! Women deserve special applause and recognition during holidays. We continue to "handle it", pull all those tiny details together, wrap, tie with a big red bow, cook, entertain, and hopefully we keep a smile on our face through it all.

Yael from Easthampton has spent over thirty years in Israel {or as she says "across the pond"} Her calling has been motivational for many men and women dealing with their own self worth and issues of survival and communication. Yael, teaches "Compassionate Listening" She shared stories of Hanukkah, A precious holiday for our Jewish friends. The festival of lights for eight days. A candle lighted each night, a gift exchanged each night with loved ones, the celebration is centered around the heart, the family the belief that a one day allotment of oil lasted for eight days. As days start to become longer bringing more light, we are all drawn to the light. My greeting to you, whoever, or whatever you believe in, "bless us one and all."

Wait For it

Reflections of Christmas past. I receive letters, but I also hit the streets and interview folks of all ages, asking them to contribute their memories to my column. My all time favorite response to my question "what is your favorite reflection?" Wait for it, here it comes! The young man I queried, responded "my own reflection in the mirror." Because the question was regarding holiday reflections, I re-directed with "did you see your reflection in a Santa costume?" The young man responded "No, of course not, you simply asked about reflections!" I love his answer! A positive response with no bells or whistles! I do believe our memories and reflections should be personal. Whatever we see in the mirror of our life is probably what we gave and what we will receive as the calendar of life chases us to the final hours of our memories. When my column is printed, another Christmas will have been celebrated. There will be the moments of glitter and sparkle, and alas, there will be the more sobering moments when angels touch our eyes and gentle tears flow briefly. It could be an old favorite Christmas carol playing on the radio, news on the internet or television about people and places in trauma, or a particularly beautiful fresh cut evergreen tree in your home, decorated for another year with ornaments made by your children throughout their school years. Children all grown up now with families of their own, starting their own collection of ornaments and their own traditions. Somehow hearing the music, unwrapping the now quite vintage ornaments always brings a memory and a tear to my eyes. This is not a sad or bad experience. It is an opportunity for me to "reflect". In a world of change, confusion, and often a sense of instability, I enjoy reflecting on the past and hoping those reflections will help me to change my own little world for the better in the future.

So let us move on to some humorous reflections! My mother loved Christmas decorations. She had to purchase them after the holiday each year at a reduced rate, because that was her financial status, and my father's request. She stashed away her bargains, never forgot where she stored them and bim bam! On Christmas she was prepared with a new theme.! Bless her, because I bought some thumb tacks a month ago and cannot remember where I put them! Now dad and my brother were the electricians. They could plug, string, different bulb colors every year for the shrubs out front, and always a "new" string of lights for the Christmas tree: bubbling candles, lighted mini globes,, lighted mini candy canes, whatever was new electrically, they found it. Well on a particular year when my nephew was about four years old, staying overnight in our Springfield house on Christmas Eve, all the "kings' men" decided to surprise him with a "real" visit from Santa. Dad and brother created flashing lights, brother ran on the roof and jingled bells, my nephew's father donned my mother's latest Christmas decoration, a life like Santa Mask!, After all of the noise and lights preceded the arrival of Santa, my nephew's father entered his bedroom wearing mother's precious Santa mask uttering a loud Ho Ho Ho!. My poor dear nephew, screamed, yelled, fled to hide in the closet and never ever would sit on Santa's lap in any department store forever after. So Ho Ho Ho, hope you had a holly, jolly, with no frightful visit from Santa!

Winter in New England

Once we survived the Halloween blast, winter in the hill towns has been rather gentle in comparison to past years. One can only wonder what spring may bring? During the past few weeks readers have shared such nice memories of love, kisses, hearts, and now it is time for "flowers". As I wait for the appearance, on a dew covered lime green spring lawn, of the first robin searching for food and nesting materials I till the soil of childhood memories. Winter in New England with short days and long nights seems cozy and restful at inception. The gardens have been put to sleep allowing us to take a break from yard work and concentrate on indoor clean up, hobbies, baking and celebrations. As the winter weeks drag on I cannot wait for "yard chores" once again! From early childhood I have enjoyed digging in the earth. I fondly remember making mud pies under a hedge of hemlocks at our city home. I had fictitious friends who loved my earthy tea parties. The big event in our home was the arrival of the seed catalogs. Dad and brother spent hours pouring through the colorful pages, making lists, drawing diagrams for planting, and finally, after some heated discussion, order forms were filled out and mailed. Then it was the women's turn to select the flowers. Mom and I spent hours at the kitchen table drooling over the amazing "State Fair Zinnias", the giant marigolds, the vibrant delphinium. A sure attraction for the tiny, gentle, hummingbirds. When the seeds arrived in the mail the excitement began again. Now each person searching through the package for their seed packets, and once again, marveling over the beauty of the picture on the packet, and dreaming of how these tiny seeds would fill our yard with beauty and food to preserve for the next winter.

Sharon from Springfield dug deeply in her memory soil and shared the following with me. Her first memory of flowers was at about age three. Each year her dad planted 75 tulip bulbs across the front of the house. Sharon, on little tip toes would gaze out the window each morning waiting to see the colorful blooms. On the first day of full bloom, Sharon said she was so excited and now so many years later, the tulips her dad planted are a favorite memory. One year a little boy across the street spent all day helping her dad plant the bulbs. The next morning the bulbs were all dug up and neatly piled. The little boy just could not STOP helping!

Hearts and Flowers

Ah yes, the old song, "Kiss me once, Kiss me twice, Kiss me once again, it's been a LONG, LONG time!" I am sure young readers will not rush to down load that song on their iPods, but for us older folks, now that I have reminded you, you may find it annoying trying to keep that melody out of your memory for the next few days. And then , KISS, "keep it simple stupid", not to mention the magic that happens in our brains when we salivate over a Hershey Kiss and pop it in our mouth and savor that amazing melting fix of chocolate! Dark chocolate in moderation now lays claim to heart and brain health, not to mention everyone's favorite, subject in 2012, libido! This is a family friendly column. On to memories of love, kisses, hearts and flowers, and trying to "keep it simple somehow". Does love start with the first kiss we ever remember? Or does love begin within our heart from birth? Is love generic? or must it be trademarked, brand-named, stamped with an OLS{official love seal from the USDA} is kissing the beginning? Or just a demonstration of our need for "touch". I share memories, but do not give advice. I am not "jack of all trades, master of none". My old buddy "Webster" defines "touch", as allowing a body part like hands to feel and come in contact with., To join, to have an effect on, to move emotionally. Close your eyes and remember your first kiss. From that memory you may be surprised about your journey through life. Who have you touched, made union with, or connected with emotionally? Who has touched you with their own "kiss?"

Recently a special lady, by nature a hugger and kisser, was invited by her companion to a family event. To her surprise, the companion's ex-wife whom she had never met, was present. At the end of the event the lady wanted to say goodbye to the ex-wife, but instinct told her not to hug and kiss! She opted for a pleasant greeting and a handshake, feeling it was a good choice. The ex-wife received the gesture with a smile and approval. Somehow, they touched each other emotionally and that is all that really matters. Kisses are accepted by all genders and even creatures. Pets need our kisses and they return to us the same. The gentle kiss of my dog or my cat is divine, Once again we are touching a living being emotionally with love. Correct me, but our sensitivity and rejection to touch could be our "lock", yet the kiss could be the secret combination through touch, to open our hearts to our most basic emotional needs, love and belonging.

A hill town gentleman expressed that his first kiss was at age 24 in the front seat of his vehicle. When I asked why he waited so long? He said he was very bashful. After dating a beautiful young lady for several months he got up the courage to "kiss". They have been married for over forty years and he has never kissed another woman on the lips. He said "it was wonderful," and he will never forget the moment and is so glad he waited to "share that first kiss with the perfect mate". How many of us can say that?

48

At about age 7, I was allowed to have a co-ed Valentine's party for my elementary school friends. My girlfriends discussed "spin the bottle" My mother agreed to have boys and girls. Spin the bottle, OK , but NO lip kissing. If the bottle pointed to a boy after the spin, I could only say "something nice" to the boy and kiss him on the cheek. I had such a crush on a boy named Walter. Three boys came to the party, one of whom was Walter. Cupid's arrow was aimed at my heart! After many spins by all guests, it was my turn, and WOW, the phone rang upstairs and mom ran to answer it and the bottle stopped spinning and pointed to Walter. I was going in for the Kiss, on the lips, when Mother returned with a tray of hot brownies, and Walter had to use the facilities. Darn! Foiled again.

Memorial Day

Continuing the theme of summer memories, we must also honor Memorial Day. My father grew up as a poor farm boy, with many memories of childhood traditions which were so unpretentious back then, but gave children such joy and expectation, excitingly awaiting the next special school or community event, having only their own creativity and limited resources to call upon. Year after year dad retold his favorite childhood memory of the school children in Russellville marching to the cemetery on Memorial Day, each child carrying a small handmade flag and a bunch of lilacs, marching quietly in reverence to the beat of one small drum. Dad said it was a "great honor" to be chosen as the "drummer boy."

The children each had an assigned gravesite to be honored with their humble decorations. After all the decorations had been placed, the "drummer boy," contributed a few soft beats: a prayer was offered; the children lined up and marched back to the school where loving parents waited to provide the children with cookies, and if it was a prosperous year for some families, there would be lemonade!

There were chores to be done because even then, Memorial Day was recognized as the unofficial beginning of summer, and crops had to be tended which meant these farm children could not dilly-dally too long enjoying recreation.

As a teenage boy, dad joined the Navy during WWI. His view of the world was expanded far beyond his humble beginnings in Russellville. After seven Voyages to France on the Matsonia he returned home an honored Veteran. During his adult life he marched into many cemeteries as a man, stepping proudly beside VFW comrades every Memorial Day, yes even with Drum and Bugle corps, and yes he was the "drummer man" when needed, but basically dad was a fiddle/saxophone man. Over the years, our family celebrated by planting crops, walking to the local cemetery to watch dad in the parade, decorating the graves of loved ones, returning home for a feast of the usual, hamburgers, hot dogs, watermelon, ice tea, lemonade, cookies, cake, and as age allowed, the spirit of our choice.

So many things have changed during the past one hundred years. As I watch television news reports, read events in the newspaper, and listen to friends and neighbors discuss their plans for Memorial Day, some traditions never change. As the saying goes "if it isn't broken, don't fix it!" However, I have no lilac blossoms. They bloomed a month ago. Guess our climate has changed!

Mother's Day

The poignant old song "MOTHER" musically and spiritually captures the feelings of most of the contributor's to my column this week. As we evolve in modern daily life, we computerize, supersize, electronically size, politicize, in our constant need as humans to improve ourselves and the world around us. We *go green*, build a better machine, communicate in text not handwriting. Even a "better mouse trap" has been created; the "heart safe" cage that captures the mouse alive, so that it may be released unharmed back into nature by a caring human.

A few years ago a friend gave me one of those traps as a Mother's Day present. Believe it or not, I was excited! I had a mouse living in the trunk of my car. Those who know me well are very aware that I have a real affection for rodents. I lovingly placed the trap in the trunk, fixating on the day I would catch the little creature and let it go! Whoops!!, forgot to check the trap. When I finally "remembered", Oh yes, it did the job, accept the poor mouse was petrified and must have passed on from starvation. Obviously the modern invention did not computerize my aging brain into a timely response.

Sometimes old things outlast the new. Instead of searching for the perfect Mother's Day gift, which may require assembling, wiring, batteries, or may wilt in a day, join me in a chorus from the good old days. Sing it out loud to your mother, may she be near or far, teach it to your children and let your memories follow the bouncing ball! MOTHER: M is for the million things you gave me: O means that you are growing old: T is for the tears you shed to save me: H is for your heart so full of gold: E is for your eyes and all their splendor: R is right and right you'll always be. Put them all together they spell MOTHER, the word that means the world to me!

LL shared memories of his mother's kiss on his check. "I do not remember her first kiss or her last, but almost every day something reminds me of her kiss. She was a stern woman, who was always RIGHT!, yet her gentle kiss reminded me of her vulnerability as a woman It taught me respect for her and all women and no other kiss has ever comforted me like hers." Sara shared: "My mother's EYES were always sparkling. Even when she cried there was hidden joy in her eyes. Now in the autumn of my life, I can still close my eyes and see hers as if she was next to me. It is empowering."

Sharon wrote: "Even as mother grew OLDER she was fearless. Travel was her passion. During the first uncertain days of Desert Storm, my mother flew to Italy to observe a young man entering into the priesthood. He had been a Sunday School student of hers many years earlier. Dad and I were worried about her safety on foreign soil. Mother said "fear not" I can do this!" Sharon wishes she too could be fearless, but lacks mother's gene.

Tam tells me she was quite a petulant child, especially in teenage years. Her mother SAVED her from many misjudgments. Her mother's heart was overflowing with forgiveness.. Tam has raised three children and has learned the meaning of her mother's famous words: "Someday when you have children of your own you will understand why I am taking this action."

Think Plastic

We cannot celebrate the start of summer without remembering the final days of the school year. The excitement in the eyes of children counting down the number of days until school is out; the thought of a homework free summer, outdoor activities with friends and family, staying up later at night, and for some older kids, a new summer job to challenge them.

For the high school or college graduate there is great preparation for the pomp and circumstance of graduation ceremonies, with "after" parties to be planned, endless advice from the oldsters to be graciously accepted, {think plastic!} There is something about seeing a graduate in their cap and gown, anxiously awaiting their name to be called, proudly walking across a stage to receive their diploma, full of hopes, dreams and a sense of freedom from studies for a bit. What can be said, it charges everyone's memory banks with a variety of emotions. For me, it is comparable to one of those slow motion scenes in the movies, with the characters gliding through a daisy filled field, smiling, drifting with the breeze, carefree, timeless.

When it is your own child receiving the diploma, one cannot help remembering the day you brought that child home from the hospital; A new tiny, helpless, tender life, wrapped in swaddling clothes, depending on his or her family for all needs. Even when it is a neighbor or friend's child, memories of watching the child grow up; building a fort or "hideout" clubhouse with my kids in our yard, running a kid's bazaar to raise money for a worthy charity. Sharing birthday parties, passing out hot cookies, bandaging a minor scrape, listening to teenage girls and their quest for beauty and boys. Staying awake until your son finished his endless homework. The memories are overflowing for most of us, and for me, I suddenly realize how old I am becoming, because it all seems like yesterday, alas it wasn't, it was years ago. Where did those years go?

Kristen from Killingworth, a 2012 college graduate, shared the following: "I have so many memories of growing up with my family, but my college friends and memories are super special." "We did some crazy things our parents may have frowned on, but mostly we were all away from home for the first time. "Four years seemed like a LONG time away from home" We all hung together through tough exams, personal dilemmas, homesickness, and shared forever memories." I now look forward to a new road ahead, building new memories, facing new challenges and being able to remember every detail so I may share with my children someday."

Sharon from Springfield had a special summertime memory :{ hello to Springfield readers! Glad you are with us!} She was about 15 and one half years old. School was out and she was cranking for a new "adult" experience. Her dad had a fully equipped late 70's Ford Econoline van, complete with a dining area that converted to a sleeping area, even a sink with running cold water, and her particular favorite, a closet for her hot teenage wardrobe. After teasing, batting her blue eyes, and begging, daddy, he agreed to drive the van, Sharon and her best new girlfriend to a campground in Otis and he would find a ride home, allowing them to spend the weekend on their own. Sharon now in her forties, still giggles like a child when she tells her story. She felt all grown up and was so happy her father trusted her so she could have this forever memorable experience.

Except for a few skunks and things that went "bump in the night" they had a fabulous time.

Fireworks

When you read this column the official 4th of July will be just another memory. It does seem that this particular holiday falling in the middle of the week creates the opportunity for two holiday weekends, before and "aft, and the possibility for multiple displays of fireworks! Not to mention family gatherings and the joy of green grass for children to play on and warm summer evenings to sit on a blanket and watch the sky light up!

For the first thirteen years of my life the anticipation and excitement of 4th of July was celebrated at our summer home, lovingly named "Singing Hills". We had an outhouse, ice chest in the cellar, hand pump in the kitchen sink, well water, an old black wood/kerosene stove for cooking and a big old fire pit outside for summer picnics. No modern conveniences but lots of fresh grown vegetables and folks came from all around for 4th of July. Dad and brother sent away for fireworks and spent hours planning the set up and safety for the displays. Mother repainted all the old lawn furniture and created quiet venues under the butternut trees where family and friends sipped the constant supply of her famous fresh squeezed lemonade and refreshing mint ice tea. Fritz M was in charge of grinding his famous hamburg, ordering pounds of hot dogs, rolls and giant watermelons for our annual celebration. If finances allowed there would be a giant pot of steamers heating up at the fire pit. In those days we had corn in the field as high as an elephant's eye ready to husk and boil for the 4th of July. Not so here in downtown Chester in 2012. We had to buy corn this week.

Guests started arriving early in the day. Relatives from out of town made long drives to be with us. City friends with vehicles which were not "dirt road worthy" often "ran aground" and dad and brother had to pull their cars out of a muddy ditch. That always created a period of frenzy for everyone, on an otherwise stress less day. As dusk moved in the anticipation for total darkness grew as we awaited the first roman candle to be fired up and fill the sky with the magic of pyrotechnics. Adults had comfortable chairs, us kids took to the grass because that was respectful, and besides who can forget the smell of grass, clover and coolness as we rolled around waiting for the next big bang and glorious overhead display of pure magic! The final presentation was a lighted American Flag and a waterfall.

In later years my family spent the 4th at Cape Cod. The Grist Mill Pond in Sandwich had a flotilla contest consisting of children and their parents decorating row boats with a variety of candles, lights and Japanese Lanterns. The boats were judged and the best boat was the winner. As the boats floated around the pristine pond, it was quiet, but just as magical as a big bang in the sky.

In the small town of Morning Sun, Iowa, everyone comes "home" for the 4th of July. Celebrations are ongoing for several days, including class reunions, a huge parade complete with tractors, horses, 18 wheelers, flower arrangement contest at the local school, church services and culminating with fireworks exploding high over the crisp green corn fields. The local Lion's Club prepares a barbecue for all to enjoy. Beef is wrapped and put in the ground in a fire pit and cooks all night. Once cooked it is pulled apart and served on wonderful homemade buns, along with salads and cold drinks. Hope you all made new memories this 4th of July.

Summer in New England

The final installment of summertime memories, for this year! If I make it through another summer I will probably subject readers to the same memory exercise once again. During the past few weeks, your response has been more than I could have hoped for. Perhaps there is something about summer in New England that is permanently etched in our memory. Is it the warm days?, the long sunsets?, the beautiful flowers?, the freedom from layers of clothing? That wonderful first glow of dawn with birds singing outside open bedroom windows, and the smell of growing grass, mowing hay fields, corn silk! {Oh yes, it has an aroma so sweet} The promise of another long day, during which many folks will enjoy the beginning of a year- long awaited vacation, or perhaps just a day off to relax and reflect and enjoy! Whatever the reason, it is personal to each of us, and inspirational when shared with others. For me, summertime in Chester reminds me of a Thomas Kinkade painting; specifically, "The End of a Perfect Day III". I have always enjoyed a non-intellectual interest in the arts. Picasso, Monet, Rembrandt, Andrew Wyeth, "Christina". There is something about Wyeth that primes a similar attraction in me to Kinkade. With Kinkade his use of luminosity, the glow of sunshine yellow in hit or miss places within his paintings. As for Wyeth, it is the rather blank, yet promising look in the eyes of the girl looking over the hill into what lies beyond. Somehow these paintings reflect my summertime of life. First I glow and then I am blank and full of my own mortality! Now, I ask you, is that not a "light at the end of the tunnel". The front porch in Kinkade's painting, as referenced above, gives way to the following: A memory from Priscilla from Hampshire County.

"In warm weather, the wrap-around front porch on our old farmhouse became the gathering place for lemonade and conversation at the end of the day. One end of the porch was supported by a large old piece of wood. It was not pretty, but it supported the sloping end of the porch. I guess Daddy would have replaced the damaged structure if he had money and energy." To me it did not matter. We all stayed on the "safe side of the porch". After dinner, as dusk wrapped around our country home, friends came a calling. The best visitors were the ones bringing instruments! "Guitars, a banjo player and oh yes a Mandolin!" "If we were lucky an old guy with a long grey beard came and blew in some jugs, creating a sound that resonated like an echo off of the surrounding mountains "Next best was the skinny guy with a washtub. It had a broomstick and one pieces of string. He kept the rhythm, which once again resonated! It felt like a heartbeat beneath the earth!" I would start to dance and jump and jig, because I could not sit still! My favorite guest was Uncle Morgan! "He never arrived without his harmonica, or as I learned later, his mouth organ. His name was not Morgan, get it?" "To this day I really do not know his "god-given-name," nor do I know if he really was my uncle! What I do remember in my ageing life is that he made the hills sing and he made me so happy to be alive." Thank you Priscilla! You must be related to me. On a back porch in my young life, the hills came alive with the sound of music and I could not stop dancing! My dad called the whippoorwill every night and the deer ate green apples in the orchard.

Part Three
Memory Soil

Long Island Boys

As we parted in my last column the three thirty year friends from Long Island had just crossed the border into Canada. It was now after 2PM on this "day trip" to Montreal for a little fun at the casino. During the long delay at Border Patrol the storm escalated and a 15 minute drive into Montreal had now become a driving nightmare with nothing but desolation on either side of the highway. The three Musketeers were not going to let a blizzard keep them from the casino, some brew and a big meal! But wait for it! *Kaboom!* Loud popping noise, truck running rough! Yep, it blew a spark plug.

Gino finds a place to pull over to make some calls to locate an auto parts store. Smart phones are smart however the guys were parked in the middle of French Canadian country and each call was answered in French, a language these boys forgot to take in school on Long Island.

The group decides to hit the road again and try to find help up ahead. Miraculously they came upon a Restaurant, Repair shop, old house with people on the front porch. Not such a miracle, everything closed at 2:00 PM because it was Sunday. The group of people, French speaking only, finally understood by the sounds coming from Gino's truck, that he had vehicle problems. Sometimes just a noise is worth a thousand words! With lots of hand signals, nodding heads, etc. directions were given to an auto parts store. The store however would close at 3:30. Gino and the boys pulled in at 3:20. Everything needed to fix the good old Ford F150 was purchased and Gino began the repair, discovering that the Ford mechanic who last worked on the truck had stripped a screw, resulting in the current dilemma. With the weather conditions now a white-out, Florida Frank was sure he was suffering from hypothermia and retreated to the inside of the truck. One last screw but Jimmy's hands were so cold he dropped it. A frantic search ensues and eventually Gino improvises and it is then the moment of truth! Yes the truck starts up, purring like the proverbial kitten! The three guys back in the truck, heater blasting, make a unified decision to turn around and head back home to the USA! The Border Patrol did not detain them on their return. Shortly after entering home soil the guys stopped for a burger and a brew. Later they stopped at a real restaurant and feasted on big dinners. Returning to camp in the wee hours of the morning they topped off their "day trip" with a nightcap, rehashed the day, laughed and decided next year they will make it to the casino. Or not! The three friends take all adventures with a cheerful attitude. All that really matters to them is spending a boys' weekend together for as many years as possible. We all need long lasting friendships. Readers are welcome to share stories of day trips with me. I have a few of my own. Some of them have the Chevy Chase Vacation theme.

BFFs

Friends, friendship, BFF? Best friends forever, or BFN, best friends now? Do some friends ride the waves of life and dock together at the same shores, or are some friends like ships passing in the night?, filling a moment in our memories, never to connect again. For Christian families, the old hymn, "What a Friend I Have In Jesus", promises ethereal, eternal, friendship. The holiday season nudges us to purchase greeting cards, update our list of family and friends, and "communicate". I have not sent cards diligently throughout my life. My excuses?; when I was younger, lack of time seemed to be a personal excuse. Then excuse number two, cards written by someone else never "maudlinly" express my feelings. Currently cost is the reason. If I made 69 friends in my life, at 44 cents for postage, plus the price of 69 cards, well it adds up. Each year I am amazed at how many dear friends still keep me on their list even though they have not received a card from me in years. At my age "happy mail" is a special treat. I am grateful to be remembered, and apologize for my excuses. I am embarrassed to admit that I have two problems with "greetings". A card without a quick note included is disappointing. A generic computer compiled letter with information about the past year, full of spectacular accomplishments and events from the sender, leaves me wondering why my year was so lack-luster?

Flo, raised in Russell, expressed her thoughts on friends. At an early age, Flo, knew which of her friends would be "forever". "It was instinctive, I felt it in first grade." "Some girls like to be "in", just like the latest fashion trend. Whoever was popular, attractive, and lived in a nice home, with nice parents, had popular parties, became the BFN. Those friends I have lost touch with. Others truly bonded with me and we still, at my age of 37, share our deepest secrets, take strength from each other during rough times, rejoice together in good times and communicate with each other frequently."

A hill town gentlemen had a best friend growing up. They shared everything for years. When his friend became extremely successful, the communication ended. The gentleman feels his old friend, Jack, would always be glad to hear from him, but Jack would never be the one to make the "first call". New Jersey has the "Situation", but Long Island boys have the "solution" to true friendship. GT from Long Island has been BFF with Jimmy and Frank since age 16. First memory "sub sandwiches" after school on Fridays transported in a 74 Malibu wagon. Trips to upstate NY for snowmobiling. Traveling in '79 Bronco that blew a rod. GT hikes to a Police Barracks, after a quick coffee, with a friendly " giant" trooper, GT is left at a U-Haul place. GT has to dig out the tow dually in three feet of snow. An hour and a half later, three friends looking through frosty windows, saying "let's go home" for Monday night football. Eventually marriages, families, and still every year the LI boys

unite for a special adventure, stay in touch during the
year, and always laugh and remember all of their
unique adventures. Thirty years later they still sing
"Stand By Me."

Road Rage

My husband had an appointment for his second cataract surgery. As we checked in to the doctor's office and waited for our turn, we took seats in a crowded waiting room of 14. Some folks were waiting to pick up a patient after surgery, some were nervously waiting for their own procedure. Some folks were shuffling aimlessly through magazines, others in soft conversation, some just gazing straight ahead perhaps wondering how their new sight would enhance their lives. A few were losing patience with the waiting process. All and all, they were a jovial group of people somehow we were all tossed together like a fresh summer salad in a" crystal bowl," each a visible ingredient in the bowl, yet each with individual flavor, coloring and zest, with one purpose, healthy eyes. As my husband's name was called and the nurse called me by name to ensure that I was the "designated driver" at the completion of his surgery, a lady asked me if I was "that memory woman". Taken by surprise, I was trying to process her question. She quickly explained that she did not live in the hill towns, but had friends she visited "in the country" and had read Maudlin Memories. As a "city" person, she expressed her fascination with the news and life style of the hill towns, especially the lack of crime and anger. She expressed what a peaceful trip it was for her on Route 20 west, once out of the city, and how lucky we were to travel from Chester to the doctor's office without super highways and "road rage".

As a "memory stealer" I thought I was in paradise. The waiting room exploded in conversation about bad drivers, road rage, sad stories of lost friends and loved ones because of driving miscalculations. Everyone wanted to share a memory, complete with their names. Unfortunately I was not "swift enough" to collect the names." I do not need to print your name, I only ask for your memory."

A gentleman from Florida told about his days as a truck driver. After several frightening experiences on the highway, he took gun safety classes and carries a handgun in his vehicle. Another NY state fellow called himself a "self proclaimed" road warrior. He is cautious and kind, BUT, when someone is on the turnpike driving 50 miles an hour in the passing lane, he becomes exasperated, flashes his lights and " gets on their tail". He also has a problem with toll booths. As he said, don't people know they need some money when they get to the booth?" A senior man told of a trip years ago on the Mass. Turnpike. He entered in Westfield, his destination the WS exit. He was doing the speed limit, calm and collected, when he was cut off by an aggressive driver. The person slowed down in front of him and jammed on the breaks. The first gentlemen then passed him again, you guessed it, car number two cut him off again and proceeded to throw cans, bottles, paper, etc., out of his vehicle, as car number one exited in West Springfield. I finally shared my story, on that very morning a person "flipped" me off because I edged over the stop line at the bridge in Huntington, not blocking any traffic. The red construction light on the bridge did not change for almost five minutes. We had plenty of time to make our appointment, but I felt the light was stuck and simply wanted to see if there was a workman on the other side of the barriers who could help. I was a tad naughty to move forward, but I was not in a hurry or angry! The gesture made me sad.

Laugh Lines

For parents in my reading audience who have adult children who live in far away places, I think you will agree with me, when the kids come home for a visit it is always a great reunion. For families who are fortunate enough to have children living nearby, we may not experience the same excitement because we see them on a daily or weekly basis. Whatever our personal situation may be, the joy of homecoming always creates new memories and tall tales to be shared with future generations. My daughter and son-in-law were home from Long Island for a brief visit and I coaxed my daughter into agreeing to be my guest writer this week. The following are her maudlin memories:

Memories are funny things. I often wonder how embellished my even truest memories actually are. My brother swears that my story of the bear in the backyard is only the result of my always active imagination. Then again (and this will be our secret) I think I've always realized that. Yet some of the smallest, most mundane memories I have are so clear; so vivid that I can actually feel them-- from the coolness of the memories of making snow angels; or the texture of that silly little toy I used to play with by the hour, to the warmth of my mother's smile when I'd look over at her as we drew pictures in the clouds, to that welcomed aching in my side that can only be brought about by the uncontrollable laughter shared with only the select few.

I am so happy to be home again in the hilltowns this weekend for my 20th Class Reunion. Wow. 20 years. It's surreal really. I can remember getting ready in my room for all those years with my AquaNet and big hair that always seemed to take hours to "fix" yet, let's face it, really only managed to look ridiculous.

Fast forward to 2012 and here I am again getting ready in that very room but today as a married woman and a working professional with THE life I had only ever imagined. I'll admit that there is a part of me that is nervous about how my hair will look, the weight I had once lost but is now found, and whether or not I should wear my purple heels or high boots. But even more so, I am anxious to relive embellished memories while creating new ones with classmates turned adults.

I've since abandoned the AquaNet and winged sides (thank you fashion Gods) and as I type here today, I can't help but think how little any of that really matters. What matters is that I know my side will ache from laughter later today, my laugh-lines will be further engrained, and memories only the hilltowns can provide will be created tonight for me to cherish until we exaggerate them together in another 10 years!

Making it to the Olympics

With the Summer Olympics in London now underway, I find myself absorbed in not only the competitive events and the desire to learn that our blessed USA has medaled, but even more I am so moved by the stories and memories of the athletes from childhood. The physical challenges, injuries, the exhausting hours of training, the meltdowns, the wins, the losses, and finally, the joy of "making it to the Olympics!" In the end it is not about the gold, it is about that wonderful human spirit to overcome all odds and be the best we can be.

Recently I had the great joy to reunite with a dear childhood friend from Russell. We shared memories, of course, because that is what I do! To my surprise and delight, my friend volunteered to write his memories. I dedicate this column to Donnie Strickland, a true man worthy of the gold! A few years ago in the prime time of his life, as a family man and a successful corporate lawyer, Donnie suffered a traumatic brain injury. His world as he knew it went in to slow motion. All of his motor skills were impaired, as well as memories. Years of rehabilitation awaited him. He now reads at a 6th grade level, can write, speak, and walk. Perhaps all of the above still in a much slower motion than we can understand. Nonetheless, he has never given up and continues to work diligently each day. The following are his memories of Russell in summertime.

"Even though there was no TV or computers in Russell in the 1950's, being a young boy it was a very active place. Just about all the men and some women worked at Westfield River Paper Co. The day would end at 4:30PM, employees carrying lunch pails, heading home! Some folks worked at Texon. Russell had three grocery stores, which was necessary because most of the women did not have cars. Friday was exciting in the Sullen family because Dad drove us to Westfield, to shop, see a movie, attend a concert in the park, and at special times, we went to a real restaurant for dinner. Mom shopped in all the local stores. She was always dressed as if she was going to a ball. She spent lots of time visiting with friends met on the streets of Westfield also on a Friday night escape from Russell. But the biggest excitement for me was the annual Memorial Day Parade in Russell. Boy and Girl Scouts, bands, children riding decorated bikes or pulling wagons dressed in red, white and blue. When the Veteran's marched at the front of the parade that gave me great joy! WWII only a few years in the past, we young guys were really into combat movies about the war and comic books about superheroes. Military men in the front of the parade in order of service: Spanish American, a small group sometimes in antique cars: WWI Vets had their own unique uniforms: The WWII vets were the largest group back in 1950. Army, Navy, Marine Corp, all these men had fought bravely to defend our country. For a young boy like me, it was magic! After the parade some of us headed for the local swimming pool. We could also walk to the local train station and watch passengers boarding for a destination of Westfield, Springfield or beyond. Yes those were the lazy hazy days of summer for a young man in Russell. I sometimes wish all young men could have gathered the same memories." Thank you Donnie, you have earned a medal from my heart!

Part Four

A Bit of Whimsy

Theatre

People we remember can be special in a variety of accomplishments. We honor them, quote them, memorialize them. This week, my son David Proctor, offers his memories of Vincent Dowling.

"I first saw Vincent Dowling at the Miniature Theatre of Chester in the summer of 1994 when Vincent was co-starring with Kim Hunter in the "The Gin Game." The theatre was housed, as it is today, in the Chester Town Hall auditorium but in 1994 there was no air conditioning, there were no risers, and it was a very hot August night. The auditorium was packed and stifling, the windows were open and you could hear the traffic on route 20. Fans were stationed on the floors in what was not an entirely successful attempt to keep the audience cool. In spite of the heat, in spite of the noise outside, the audience, myself included, sat transfixed by the performance on stage. Vincent had the audience in the very palm of his hand. Every emotion—joy, rage, love—that Vincent's character experienced we (the audience) felt, we were not just observers, we were in the play. The heat, the noise, none of it mattered to me that night. That was Vincent's power as an actor, he could not only make you believe he was the character he was portraying on stage, but he could erase any boundary between audience and actor, he had the ability to transport you into the very fabric of the play, allowing you to experience the performance from within.

In June of 1996, a little under two years after that August night, I was hired as the box office manager for the MTC. Vincent had stepped down at the end of the previous season as Artistic Director, but Olwen Dowling was still serving as Managing Director and Vincent was still very much involved in the theatre. For the next six years I served as box office manager and then director of box office operations, and had the opportunity to work with and get to know Vincent Dowling. In one of my first meetings with Vincent after joining the staff, he shared with me his view that theatre was much more than just entertainment, it was a window on humanity and the human condition and was something that everyone should have the opportunity to experience, that theatre could have a real impact on people's lives. This was a perspective that Vincent not only believed, but one I saw him continually put into action both through the plays he argued should be performed and by his ongoing and unshakeable belief in the need for the theatre to reach out to the hill town communities—to families, to senior citizens, to students—to everyone. His efforts transcended the Miniature Theatre and included a variety of performances in venues of all shapes and sizes as well as an almost unceasing string of personal appearances, talks, community events and fundraisers for local organizations.

Vincent would never refuse a request to share his talents, his knowledge and his passion for what theatre and the written word could mean and what it could achieve.

The last show I worked on with Vincent came in 2008 when I served as box office manager for the Vincent Dowling Theatre Company's performance of "The Rivalry." This was a play Vincent deeply believed in, not only because it made the debates between Abraham Lincoln and Stephen Douglas come alive, but because he fundamentally believed it had a message that was powerfully relevant to the political rhetoric in 2008. I remember distinctly how gratified Vincent was when he met one young audience member. A young man around 10 who was being homeschooled, who saw the play several times during its run in Chester including having his mom bring him to a performance for his birthday. For Vincent, that was what it was all about."

Content

Happy: contentment; Happiness: the quality of being content; Happy-go-lucky: being not worried about what may happen. All of the above, our memory exercise for this week, and like our childhood devotion to fairy tales, we all love a "happy ending".
CS from Franklin county shared the "cat came back story."

Her beloved cat, "fluffy" vanished on a cold autumn day. Having been a member of the family home for over a decade, and never having strayed from the yard, CS was devastated when dusk approached and "fluffy" did not respond to the suppertime call. Fluffy was a hearty eater and never missed meal call! CS took to the streets calling Fluffy's name over and over again. A group of kind neighbors took up the search. As the darkness surrounded the search party and the cold autumn winds gained strength, the search ended for the night. CS left the porch light on, just in case. As the wind howled through the night, CS could not sleep. With every noise she was sure it must be Fluffy returning home to chow down, wash up, and stretch out once again in her favorite spot by the wood stove... Days, weeks, months passed. Time passing does heal our losses in life, but our devotion to those we love when departed from us leaves a void. Also old habits die hard. For CS she occasionally would forget and call Fluffy to come for supper. As human's

we all seem to require answers to our mysteries. That modern saying; we need closure! For CS the wondering where Fluffy had gone, was she still alive? was she warm and safe? Had she found a new home and if so, why would she want one? The wondering was more painful than the absence of her pet.
Over a year passed, and yes it was late afternoon on a cold autumn day when a faint "meow" was heard at the back door. CS was afraid to respond, thinking her imagination was playing one more trick on her. CS approached the door with heavy, slow steps. Yes, yes! it was FLUFFY!!, looking a bit older, a bit tattered and torn, skinny, but alive and home again. Although the mystery of Fluffy's disappearance will never be known, CS exclaims with such joy that the return of Fluffy was and will be her happiest memory ever.

An anonymous reader shared a similar story but quite the opposite. She had what she describes as {not my words} a nasty old cat, who also will remain anonymous. She writes that he killed birds at her feeder, clawed her furniture, scratched and bit family and friends. One day "anonymous" vanished never to return. The writer says that was her happiest day ever!

Once the table is set and the turkey is in the oven, I will be BonnieAnn Happy-go-lucky! I will be content! My happiest memories will always be about family and friends gathering together for any occasion sharing stories, sparing gently about political, worldly issues, playing music and embracing the precious moments of life. Two gentlemen shared the same happy memory, individual to each of them. Guess what ladies out there? They both one age 40, one age 76, said their wedding day was the happiest memory of their lives! Now in this day and age of "sorted abandon affairs of the heart," that is a happy, happy memory! Thanksgiving blessings to all from me to you!

Year of the Zombie

During our lifetime we have heard of the Chinese calendar referencing the year of the horse, goat, monkey, rat, etc. Well kids from my sources on the "spider's web", for Halloween in 2012, here in the USA, wait for it... this is the year of the ZOMBIE! Because I always do my research, I checked with my old pal" Webster": Zombie: "person who resembles the walking dead". Ok, that is not enough for me. I now checked with a neighbor who was a mortician for several years. I asked him if he ever witnessed a dead person walking? Never was his answer! Oh my ghostliness! If I had young children today I would not know where to begin with one of my homemade costumes You see, I always need a point of reference before I begin a creative endeavor. According to television reporters and internet sources, Halloween is a BIG commercial profit making event, only to be outdone by Christmas. Of course Christmas generally includes a big gift and "stocking stuffer". Once upon a time, Halloween only required an old sheet, pillow case and the benevolence of the folks who answered a knock on their door and provided, apples, popcorn balls, homemade cookies and brownies to the trick-or-treaters. I guess we could up the anti with ghost and pumpkin stuffers, but then again, all treats must be hermetically sealed making homemade gifts a no-no at Halloween. Apparently the greatest cost at Halloween is not the mini wrapped sweets that are given out at the door. The big money is spent on costumes and lawn decorations. In case you are inventive enough to create your own Zombie costume for your little one, you must buy black zombie blood to ensure the accuracy of the costume. Because at any age we all know Zombies are dead so they will not drip red blood. Not like the old days of Dracula who only sucked the real hi-test stuff.

G shared his memory. He and his sister wore costumes which consisted of a pillow case with eyes cut in it, tied around the neck with jute. Another pillow case in hand to collect the goodies. After a jolly good night of treating, his mom dumped the contents on the kitchen table and everyone indulged their sweet tooth. Cindy picked up on the paper mache theme and remembers her siblings working diligently for days with their mom's help, creating not only masks, but unique creations like full 4ft tall tomb stones to cover their bodies from head to toe{although difficult to walk in}.Many of you shared your stories of homemade witch and ghost costumes. All created with love and sharing with your child but very little cost involved. Mary shared her story of the headless horseman, an all time favorite for her and her son. Oh Mary, I made that costume with my son. What fun we had. My mom had an old wig form and we covered it with silly putty and painted on the features and placed on a silver tray. Actually when my son arrived in the kitchen with no head, dressed in black, carrying the "head" on a silver tray, I was a tad nervous. It was scary. What was not scary was the cost, zero..just time and love. Pat's memory is precious. Her little brother was dressed as a mummy. Because money was limited, cheap bathroom tissue had been used to wrap and tie him into this believable Halloween character. Her brother was well potty trained but still very young and concerned. Before he left for his big trick-or-treat adventure, he announced to his family, that he felt very safe because if he had a bathroom accident, he had plenty of tissue! Love it, because that is the way it was long ago.

Disclaimers

Have you noticed that multiple products and services offer a "disclaimer" in very small print? On television when a lawyer is offering dedicated and spectacular response because you had a motorcycle accident that caused great harm and or injury, call whoever and receive your fair settlement. If you ingested a particular medication which caused a series of physical malfunctions, call whoever for settlement. However in small print at the bottom of the screen, the "disclaimer." If you wish to borrow cash, sell your gold, remortgage your home, side your house, buy a fence or a new mattress, the "disclaimer." The message is on and off in a heartbeat and so small in font that perfect vision could not discern the message. In packaging of many products, {also in tiny print in a place one would never read} for weight control, hair loss, amnesia, ambrosia, arthritis, erection, injection, infection, money, or purchasing flea, tick and heartworm products for our pets: wait for it!, the disclaimer. Once we have read the basic "big print message", somehow the small print becomes less important. Newspapers use multiple fonts, however the goal is to report the news, be it BIG or small. Within that process, I proclaim a disclaimer for "Maudlin Memories," my column can only be printed when there is space. News from many hill town areas has priority, as it should have. My column is not news, it is intended only for your reflections, sharing and happiness. Thank you for missing my column during the past few weeks. Be mindful that during that time you were receiving real news from a paper dedicated to the wants and needs of its subscribers. When there is space, Maudlin Memories will have a place.

Henry from the hill towns shared an ageless memory, continuing to give him joy in his seventies. The house wren. At about age three Henry remembers awakening to the gentle, yet persistent song of the wren. At a young age the song was a wake up call, to which Henry did not want to obey. The tiny bird was resilient and had his way. As Henry aged and continued to respond to his feathered friend's alarm clock he found a bright new day awaiting him. Many years later, when the wren sings, Henry rises without annoyance, knowing another day awaits. A neighbor finds the wren's vocalization annoying. Henry finds the sweet song a gentle call to another day of life.

Lettuce Soup? It sounds like a children's book. In a Greek family it was and will be an ageless memory. A story shared by a professor from the eastern part of the state. When financial times were barren in a family home, nourishment was still important. For a family joining America with limited finances, lettuce soup filled the tummies and pleased the palate. With a tad of freshly ground ginger and a sprig of dill, served with some special bread, it was a "good thing". I share this in memorial to Prof.M from Tuft's University, whose life will be celebrated in a memorial service on Sunday. Lettuce is forever, and so are his many contributions to the world of academia, and his story about Napoleon. Safe journey!

Part Five
Red Sandals

Red Sandals

Ever so many years ago I wore tiny red sandals with punched out holes that were shaped like daisies. Every year I got a new pair (maybe.)

I knew I was a "lady" because I wore dresses with polka dots or pinstripes, sometimes checks or plaids; maybe even flowers and bows.

I ran in my sandals: I was almost always running. Sometimes I would trip, fall down, and skin my knees in my red sandals. Daddy would get upset and say "Watch where you are going or SLOW DOWN!" Mamma would put black ointment and a snow white bandage on my knees and I would wear my wounds like a bandage of honor!

I chased butterflies and bumblebees; I picked flowers and caught toads in my red sandals. I ran after my daddy and my brother across the field, under the apple trees, when they were going to the garden or hunting, all the while calling "Wait for me. Wait for me. I want to go with you!!

I DANCED in my red sandals when daddy's fiddle made my toes and my hips wiggle and swing. I played paper dolls, read Golden Books and watched rain drops on the window panes in my red sandals.I gazed at the stars, looked for the big dipper and the the little dipper and made wishes on shooting stars in my red sandals.

I blew bubbles, flew kites, and caught fireflies. I searched for nuts, berries and four leaf clovers... in my red sandals.

I sang and put on shows while dressed in sweet smelling summertime ferns that pickled my body. I gave my mommy and daddy and sister and brother kisses and said prayers... in my red sandals.

I wore my red sandals to my tea parties with my mommy, dollies, stuffed animals, and anyone else who would come to play.

I cried in my red sandals when a thorn pierced my toe Or a bee stung me. I laughed in my red sandals on hot August days when I would lie on my back watching the clouds as the long grass tickled my back.

Sometimes I pouted in my red sandals when the grownups had plans or conversations that did not include me.

I learned to make pie and jelly with my beautiful sister and sat on the piano bench with her while her fingers flew across the black and white keys... in my red sandals.

...And my red sandals waited for me by my bed each night as the Sparkle People played and I drifted off into the magic of dreamland and the expectations of a brand new day. .

I said prayers in my red sandals and one day I met Jesus and he had sandals too. I thought that was real cool... I asked him. "Jesus do you ever get a thorn in your toe?" He said "it only hurts a little" and he was gone in a heartbeat.

His dress was longer than mine and it didn't have polka dots or pinstripes and his sandals were brown and they didn't have have punched out daisy shapes on them.

But I knew it was the sandals that took us where we needed to be so I never let go of the "man with the sandals;" I wished he could stay longer and visit and maybe have tea.

***

105

When I saw her I missed a beat on my instrument because beside her stood the man with the brown sandals only for on beat and he was gone; but he smiled at me as she smiled at me and she started to dance to our music in her red sandals and her smile and her filled my world.

I felt overwhelmed with memories and energy and thankfulness. None of this is really about the shoes; I guess more it about our life, our faith, our spirit and our Lord.

The memory of my red sandals and meeting a member of a newer generation in red sandals gives me faith in the promise of each new generation, the promise of life ever after, and the glory of each new day of our earthly life.

I do wonder what a pair of size 8 1/2 red sandals with punched out holes in a daisy design would do for 61 year old?

Part Six

The After Glow

The Afterglow

I was born in Springfield, Massachusetts. My brother Roland was nineteen when I was born and entering WWII. He named me Bonnieann. My sister Joyce was sixteen and following a lifelong career of entertaining on the 88 keys. I was called "a change of life baby" back in those days. I attended elementary school and Jr. HS thru 1955 in Springfield. At age 13 my parents were retiring and moved to Russell, MA. I attended Westfiled HS and graduated from there.

I worked for a local florist for all four years of high school and on call after I graduated. I was trained in floral design in Harford. In June 1959 after high school graduation I was accepted at a business comptometer school in Springfield. I traveled back to Springfield five days per week and graduated for business school in January 1960. I then became employed as a billing clerk in Springfield. From there I moved to fi nancial assists nt At a large Springfield fuel injection hydraulics manufacturer. Attended two more business schools five times week. Graduated from both. After five years I entered the employment counseling field with nationally franchised company located in Springfield. Eventually I worked my way closer to home and spent five years as a secretary to a state senator in Westfield. I raised two wonderful children performed part time Jobs while they were young I and eventually returned to full time employment in special education a t Gateway Regional in Huntington, MA. After a few years I moved into the central office as Treasurer/Accounts Payable. During these years I called and asked to apply back in Springfield for a job as director of administrative services. I was hired and driving 64 mile round trip. route once again.

After four wonderful years at this job, the Springfield office closed. My Children were in college by this time. I was asked to move a book of business to the South Shore and live there one year. I accepted and traveled home to my husband and family every Friday .At the end of the year I was unemployed for the first time. I attempted to market some crafts and worked at a local store with a lunch counter. I was in charge of the menu. Shortly thereafter, the business manager at Gateway called to say that my old job was open again and would I please come back. I was employed back in Hunting ton for another nine years until that job was eliminated. I th en went back to school for medical training as a Certified Nursing Assistant (CNA.) I graduated after a year, passed my state certification.

After a few months working in nursing homes, I secured a position in the medical surgical unit of a local hospital. After several years there health issues required me to take a vocational vacation. I finally had the opportunity to write, however in addition, a wonderful band, Country Frie ndship asked me to join them with my big "dog house" bas s fiddle. We played for every imaginable event. I dropped the writing once again. When the band dissolved because of the passing of the founders of the band, I returned to writing once again.

I have two precious children a son David and a daughter Miriam. They put themselves through years of college. They are both married and successful young adults, following their dreams and challenges everyday. I live with my husband, our faithful beagle and robust cat in a small town in the Berkshires, known as the "gem of the valley." It has always been my dream to publish a book of inspiration; one that is soft and fluffy, fun and family; one that would evoke a few tears, many laughs. It is my hope that *Maudlin Memories* will provide a family friendly, easy read that will challenge its readers to open their memory banks and share their experiences with the next generation.